DINO-HOCKEY

LISA WHEELER

ILLUSTRATIONS BY BARRY GOTT

For Matt, Bobbie, Tyler and Evan
Harget, with love, from aunt Lisa
— L. W.
for Rose
— B. G.

TO
ICE

www.scholastic.ca

ISBN 978-1-4431-0489-0
School Market Edition, published 2010 by Scholastic Canada Ltd.
Published by arrangement with Carolrhoda Books, a division of Lerner Publishing
Group, Inc.

6 5 4   Printed in Malaysia 108   14 15 16 17

The game begins at half past six,
when dinos grab their hockey sticks.

They play to win on icy floors—
MEAT-EATERS vs. **VEGGIESAURS!**

As their coaches shout advice,
red and green teams take the ice.

Socks and jerseys keep them warm—
cold-blooded beasts in uniform.

T-EATERS—RED TEAM

T. REX—CENTER

TROODON—GOALIE

PTERODACTYL TWINS—WINGERS

ALLOSAURUS—DEFENSEMAN

RAPTOR—DEFENSEMAN

VEGGIESAURS—GREEN TEAM

TRICERATOPS—CENTER

ANKYLOSAURUS—GOALIE

DIPLODOCUS—WINGER

APATOSAURUS—WINGER

IGUANODON—DEFENSEMAN

STEGOSAURUS—DEFENSEMAN

Safety pads protect their bones.

Some have helmets of their own.

It's T. Rex and Triceratops.
The two face off. The game puck drops.

Then dinos battle for control.

Who'll be first to score a goal?

Veggiesaurs have got the puck!
Stego licks his stick for luck.

Tricera slips. He spins. He reels!

Watch out—check! And Raptor steals!

Raptor passes to **T. Rex**.

The goalie waits for what comes next.

T. Rex shoots! He almost missed.
Hooray for Raptor—an assist!

But naughty **Pterodactyl** twins slashed the **Diplo** in the shins.

Dodo is the referee.

The red team has a penalty!

The lines are drawn up in the stands,
split by **Meat** and **Veggie** fans.

The twins fly by on hockey skates.
Apatosaurus hesitates.

T. Rex's pass is sure and quick,
received by Raptor's hockey stick.

Raptor doesn't miss a beat.
Shoots the puck at Ankylo's feet.

Ankylosaurus makes a save!
Excited sports fans do the wave.

Another faceoff. Veggies rule! Allosaurus starts to drool.

Tries to check, but she's too slow.
The toothy fans shout, "Go! Go! Go!"

Diplo and Apatosaur
move the puck across the floor.
Diplo aims. He shoots. He scores!
Hooray! A point for Veggiesaurs.

The score is tied now, 1 to 1.
The winner could be anyone.

The centers face off, nose to nose.

The puck is dropped between their toes.

Tricera sweeps. He gains control.
The Veggiesaurs are on a roll!

Iguano tries to clear the way
as Veggies keep the puck in play.

Stego's checked against the boards.
Oh no! It's dueling dinosaurs!

The two defensemen start to fight.
No fair! That **Raptor** tried to bite!

That's no way to win the cup!
The ref skates in to break things up.

Stego fumes inside the booth,
as Raptor searches for his tooth.
While Stego gripes and Raptor groans,
Triceratops is in the zone.

He knows the game's not over yet—
a slapshot!—headed for the net.

Troodon makes a dive to block.
He slips and falls just like a rock.

His save is late. His form is lame.

The **Veggiesaurs** have won the game!

They've never won the cup before!

Fans grab the players—lift them up.
Tricera holds the winning cup.

As cameras flash,
the Veggies cheer.
The season's over
for the year.

But never fear . . .

Buy your tickets! Don't delay.
Dino-Soccer starts today!